For Pat and Ron

First published in Great Britain in 2017 by
Andersen Press Ltd., 20 Vauxhall Bridge Road,
London SW1V 2SA.

First edition.

British Library Cataloguing in Publication Data available.
ISBN 978-1-78344-537-0

REECE WYKES

I DARE YOU

Andersen Press

I'm bored.

I dare you...

to eat this bug!

Well, I dare you...

to eat this bird.

Right. I dare you...

to eat this rock.

OK.
I dare you...

to eat
this tree.

DONE. I dare you...

to eat ME!

You look bored.